THE LITTLE RED ENGINE GOES TO TOWN

Pictures by

Leslie Wood

Story by

Diana Ross

D1347314

ANDRE DEUTSCH
CLASSICS

First published in Great Britain in 1952 by Faber and Faber Ltd.

This edition published in 1999 by André Deutsch Classics.

ISBN 0 233 99404 1.

"Let us have an exhibition," said An Important Person in London. "We will show what people do, we will show what people make. We will get an Organiser to plan it all." So they did.

"We must show how people travel and carry things about," said the Organiser. "Since the days when cave men dragged things by hand, to the jet-propelled aircraft we have today."

So a letter was sent to the Head of the Railway.

"Let us have some engines for our Exhibition of Transport. We want your fastest engine, your biggest engine, your oldest engine and an ordinary, everyday engine."

"Well, the first three are easy enough," said the Head of the Railway. "But what about the last one? We have thousands of everyday engines, and think of all the bad feeling if we pick only one."

"Why not choose that Little Red Engine so recently honoured by His Majesty?" suggested the senior Clerk. "It is certainly quite ordinary, but it has something special about it. The other engines

can't be jealous if we choose the Royal Red."

"The very thing," they all agreed. So a letter was sent to
Taddlecombe, asking the stationmaster to send up the Royal Red
for special duties, and it must bring its own driver. "You will travel
by night when the main lines are not too busy."

The Little Red Engine had never been out at night. The moon was rising and the stars were shining when it came from the engine shed, and went puffing along the line.

"TWOO HOO WHOO," cried a great white owl, flying from the ruins of the old granaries. "Twoo Hoo Whoo. Where are you going?"

"I am going to London to the Great Exhibition. I am part of the show. And who are you? I've never seen you before," cried the Little Red Engine.

"I'm the white owl. I fly by night. TOWOOO." And away it flew.

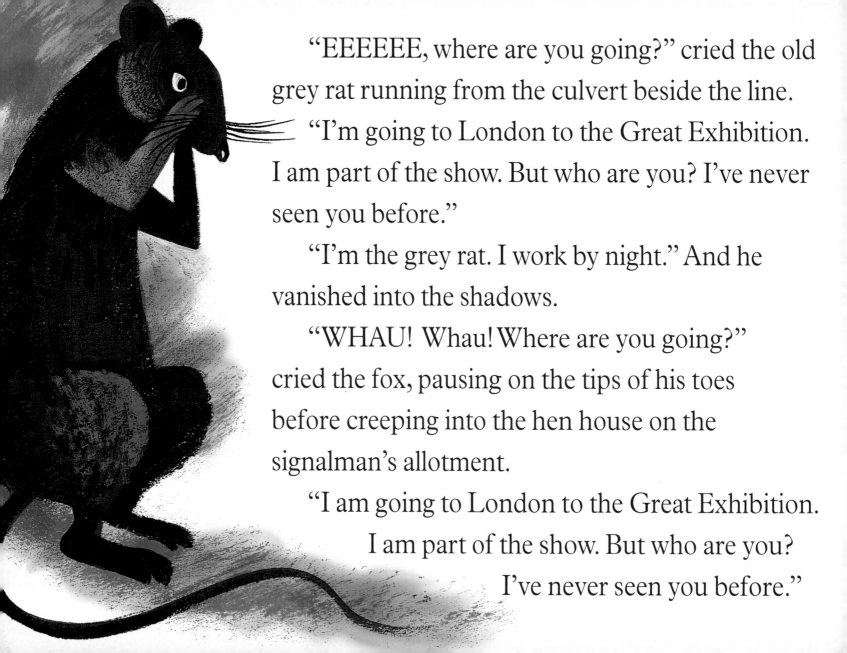

"EEEEEE, where are you going?" cried the old grey rat running from the culvert beside the line.

"I'm going to London to the Great Exhibition. I am part of the show. But who are you? I've never seen you before."

"I'm the grey rat. I work by night." And he vanished into the shadows.

"WHAU! Whau! Where are you going?" cried the fox, pausing on the tips of his toes before creeping into the hen house on the signalman's allotment.

"I am going to London to the Great Exhibition. I am part of the show. But who are you? I've never seen you before."

"I'm Reynard the fox. I hunt at night." And he jumped the wire netting.

"Where are you going?" said a tiny little voice, coming from a spark on a blade of grass. "You make a fine glow up there."

"I'm going to London to the Great Exhibition. I am part of the show. And who are you? I've never seen you before."

"I'm the glow-worm. I shine by night." And it crept away towards a thistle.

But as they got nearer to London Town there were fewer creatures to be seen, only the moonlight on the roofs of houses and the rush and roar and brightness of the night expresses thundering by.

They came into London as the morning star grew pale, but they did not go to the main platforms but were switched over to the lines which led to the repair shops.

"Why, there's nothing wrong with me, they've made a mistake," said the Little Red Engine. But it wasn't a mistake.

In the repair shops were enormous cranes. The Little Red Engine was drawn up beneath one, huge grappling irons were fastened to it, it was slowly lifted into the air, up, up, up, and then swung round, and gently down, down, down, until its wheels rested again on the solid boards of a huge trailer. The Little Red Engine shivered. "Whooooo. If that's what it's like in the air, thank goodness I wasn't made an aeroplane."

And now the trailer was hitched to a lorry and slowly they drove through the early morning streets. It was very quiet and very empty. There were only a few cats about, a street cleaner or two, and here and there a policeman.

They had to go a roundabout way as many of the roads were up. This was lucky for the Little Red Engine, which saw more of London than it would otherwise have done. It went by

Westminster Abbey where all the kings are crowned, and through Parliament Square where Big Ben chimed four. In Trafalgar Square it thought the fountains were duck ponds, and then it went past St. Paul's, but it couldn't see the apple tree as thick with apples as can be. At Tower Bridge it had to stop.

The two halves of the bridge were raised to let a steamer and a tug with barges go by. At last it came to the Exhibition gardens. The great gates were opened and it drove into the grounds.

There it saw all kinds of wonderful buildings, large and small, solid and flimsy, some like little palaces, some like houses in dreams, such buildings as were never seen in Dodge or Mazy or even Taddlecombe itself. They came to the Palace of Transport, so huge that several of the villages on the Little Red Engine's line could have fitted into it lock, stock and barrel. It was lifted on to the stand and then it looked around. It could hardly believe it. The whole huge building was full of mechanical wonders.

A real aeroplane was suspended from the roof. The very first bicycle stood next to the fastest car in the world, a Wizard Jaguar 563; a coracle made of sticks and pitch was floating in an artificial

lake and a midget submarine was alongside. And as for the engines! There were huge, shining engines far bigger and grander than the Big Black Engine Pride o' the North, and the Big Green Engine Beauty of the South which lived with the Little Red Engine at Taddlecombe, and goodness knows that they were grand enough! The Little Red Engine looked modestly at the Golden Arrow which said "How do you do?" with a foreign accent, because it went right over the sea to France.

"Say, Buddy – you look kinda dazed," said a huge engine made in England for the Canadian Pacific Railway. It had a cowcatcher in front of it so it could push out of the way any careless moose or cow which strayed on the lines as it roared through the forests and prairie lands of Canada.

"I feel rather dazed, too," said a little old-fashioned engine,
one of the first engines to be built. "When I was young my driver
wore a top hat and the women wore crinolines, and a man walked

in front of us carrying a flag. We never thought our descendants would look like this. But you look more familiar than most." And the Little Red Engine made friends with the Little Old Engine and they agreed that life in the country doesn't change so much as life on the great main lines.

The day before the Opening Day all the Organisers came to see that everything was as it should be.

They passed through the Palace of Transport.

"You know," said one of the officials, who had three little boys at home, "I think if children were allowed to go in the cab of an engine, to touch all the levers and be told how they work, I think it would please and instruct them."

"Impossible," cried the Chief Engineer. "The exhibits are Objects of Value. Children … *Touching* …? Outrageous!"

He was a single man. He didn't even keep pets, but grew prize tomatoes instead.

"But all the exhibits are not so very valuable. That little country engine, the Royal Red over there. I'm sure there could be no objection."

"Indeed, and there couldn't," cried the Head of the Exhibition.

He had five sons and two daughters, and all very fond of getting into things and touching things. "The idea is excellent. Tell the driver of the Royal Red he must be on duty throughout the Exhibition to show it to the children."

How pleased the driver was, and how pleased was the Little Red Engine. And the very next day the Exhibition was opened.

The King came with all his family, and the Lord Mayor came and all his family, and all the grand people of London and all their families and all the ordinary people of London and all their families and all the visitors from the country and all their families, and all the visitors from foreign lands and all their families, and the Little Red Engine thought all the people in the world were there.

As soon as the opening ceremony was done and the bands had

stopped playing and the
people cheering, the King
turned to his family.

"Well, now we are free to do as
we like. Where would you like to begin?"

"I want to go in the engine we can go in," cried the

youngest Prince. At first he hadn't wanted to go to the Exhibition as it meant having his gloves on - but they had told him of the Engine he could go in and then he had made no fuss at all.

"Well, it seems that you know what you want," said the King, smiling. "So we may as well start there."

Then they all moved off and came to the Little Red Engine.

The little Prince was lifted up and put in the cab. He pulled all the levers and twiddled all the knobs and smelled the oily smells, and opened the furnace door and polished the brass with the wash leather and asked a thousand questions.

"I like the Royal Red. Why is it called the Royal Red? I wish I could drive it! Do you think I could learn to drive it? Could I drive it when I'm grown up? Could I be an engine driver when I grow up?" "Perhaps," said his mother, smiling and lifting him down. Then the Lord Mayor's grandson got in and pulled all the levers and twiddled all the knobs and smelt the oily smells and opened the furnace door and polished the brass with a wash leather and asked a thousand questions.

"Can I be an engine driver when I grow up?"

"Perhaps," said the Lady Mayoress, lifting him down.

Then all the other children lined up in a long, long line, and they each got in one at a time, and they all pulled the levers and twiddled the knobs and smelled the oily smells and opened the furnace door and polished the brass with the wash leather and asked a thousand questions. And they all said they wanted to be its driver and asked if they could be engine drivers when they grew up, and each mother smiled and said "Perhaps," as she lifted down her child.

And then at the end of the day, when they

had seen everything and done everything, the Queen asked the little Prince what he had liked the best of all.

"Oh! The Little Red Engine, of course," he cried. "I'm going to be its driver when I grow up."

And as they went home each mother asked her child, "Well, and what did *you* like the best of all?"

And each replied, "The Little Red Engine, of course. I'm going to be its driver when I grow up."

And the Little Red Engine smiled to itself and quietly whistled, "Perhaps."

THE
END